On a Hill.

ON a HILL

by
M. WEISGERBER

The Detroit Publishing Company

Sunset, skydeath; every day there then went forth that orb to boil, then perish - now overhead, so soon to slip behind the West German slopes where both beauty and old tales seemed to churn in out in equal earnest.

Mitch stood there feeling a bit grizzled, once more checking his watch as he glanced up at the mass of land and the foliage that rose further east, wondering again why he should be here at this particular place, thinking of meandering such a steep peak as the one before him. The very ground around seemed made of tree roots or of broken gravel, thick ribbons that would snatch quick to his untested boots. There was still time though to get up somewhere to see something beautiful he supposed, still a few hours by which catch a quick peek, a road beer, or even make it down to one of the haughtier clubs before the city rolled its sidewalks up for the eve. He was glad he had come on this trip alone, pleased to leave his annoyances back stateside, thrilled to try something gorgeous, something green, something with terrain, something new.

He snapped a few pictures of the locals as he went up, debating his next course, amused at the bright colors and refined dress of those he passed. For he was Freiburg, and had been happy to find the city as charming as its inhabitants were bold, youthful. It was true that his legs had been getting a bit tired wandering through the town all day, checking out the larger of the Rhineland malls, nibbling upon quality links, the pastries, wondering every now and again that everyone seemed to be wearing sharp hats, or else showing their midriffs (even as he sported his own new shapely Tyrolean). Yet his eyes had not grown tired of the sights, or the loveliness being displayed in hundred thousand unnamable forms – of the people that flowed through town as easy as its legendary *bachle*, or the words and babble that seemed to bubble everywhere.

Though he was not much of a hiker, he was also smitten by the little paths that split from the town towards the parks, toward nature, figuring that the best images, the greatest future slideshows might lie somewhere up

,beyond through the bows. Better to get in shape now, he figured.

It had been hard enough to make it even this far though, as there had been several wonderous sights to distract him. The first had been a lovely biergarten carved out of some old townhouse on the lower flank of the same hill, with views out over a small garden, of vineyards flowing out to the north. How that had been difficult to leave behind, indeed. Then had been an actual park (a *platz* he had to remind, to correct himself) on the middling flanks, with fascinating dancers, the heat of the fleeting sun and enough reds and pinks and twirls swirling round to bewilder a mind. Gods, they were staggering he thought, snapping a few reams of it all, of the near cathedral seeming now to be directly at eye level. Several of the lither gals were prancing about now, with strange symbols on their clothes, their arms, hell, even their very hair seemed tasseled into unique waves, bands about the shoulders shimmering as they moved.

Best to go up, move on then.

Schlossburg. What a strange name for a hill – he would have to look into its history more later, but for now struggled with the steep quality of the upper turns, pushing past all the lounging locals, the sunburned tourists, all on his way up up up. He had seen a vantage tower on both his tourist map and listed in a highlight search of his mobile, each of which offered considerable promise - another lovely spot to watch what was sure to be a spectacular sunset, all to add to his own collection of endless images for few hapless souls back home to click at, gander, to possibly share.

Sunset. Oh how he loved sunsets; the turn of the colors upon the green, upon rock, something about the beauty of it all. He had missed seeing the one yesterday when he arrived, gazing out only into deep shadows from the flat cavern of the train depot, while waiting for the tram into town. But not today. Ahead of him was the real start of the *Schwarzwal,* the Black Forest, real monsters of trees seeming to grow and peer down. Of the stairs and stairs of stairs spread out at all angles between, stepping stones too that were covered in swooping A's and O's, with little written "B"s and curly q's seeming all around.

Gods, how the graffiti seemed to be on everything.

And damns, how his luck never seemed to hold! Ahead of him now was a bridge, one that clearly did not show on either map. It was an old thing, had clearly been rotted out for quite some time - the main central ties had all collapsed from the wet or the rain, leaving only some metal chunks apparently, some side supports still in its place. It too was covered with similar graffiti swoops and emblems that seemed to decorated the flat walls, all the sidewalks in the town below, leaving Mitch feeling a bit annoyed he hadn't noticed such sights earlier. He looked again at his mobile, then up to the sky ahead, wondering what other challenges might still be in store.

The hell with it. He clutched his pack a bit tighter, moving closer to the nearest cracked boards. He knew what Kate would have said at such an attempt, so started forward with a gleeful smile as he threaded his way across. He almost slipped twice as he went, moving slowly, grazing himself mildly on one of the nearer struts, thinking the whole time of tetanus. He made it across with no real trouble though beyond that first spell and after pouring some rum on the wound, realized it wasn't much more than an abrasion after all.

Gods though, he felt stoned. Likely, it was just the first real strain of the day, the first real exertion of locked muscles on the entire trip. *Got to get in shape, buddy boy,* he thought to himself, either for tonight, or else when he got back to the Chesapeake. That climb was no help, yet he'd have to be diligent if he wanted to stick to his plans. Higher and higher he meandered still, seeing more unusual sights as he tried to catch his breath. A giant cross of wood, double the height of a man peeping off on the right. Little playscapes, where children pranced mostly naked. Graffiti on darn near everything, befitting of the best New York dens. Even a few fake tombstones, rotten benches, flat walls poking from the very stain of earth.

Then this one in front of him.

ABNOBA. He did his best to take shots of it all, wondering what it could be, or could be later arranged, or meant. A white stone was there at odds with the green and shadows rising all around, with one single word carved brazenly into its hard side, pulling him to pause. For some reason it spoke to him, almost vibrated in a manner similar to the way the French girl had down in the platz. He wondered why this totem should stand out, all in strait letters, seeming so very Latin in this woodland layout. It was on one of the cleaner stones, looking well cared for, except for this one strange word or phrase that stood so out of place amongst the green.

ABNOBA. He started to wander on, trying his best to ignore the scribbles gathering round. There had been similar (identical?) numerals or names painted on some of the crossings back in town he remembered, in similar goofy letters or styles. It looked like someone had tried to write the word 'abnormal', and then had given up halfway through.

ABNOBA. He shook his head, to clear himself. He had to keep going, had to push a little harder if he was to catch the sunfall. Still more up then, to the tower.

He snapped a few more shots though, just in case, to check for a match, then headed still higher.

Ah, there he was! After a little longer than the map had shown in his hands, here was a burst of change. The trees had suddenly flown back, revealing a sandy grey tilted totem amongst their midst. Ahead was tubular tower that bent in a way he almost recognized, all of dulled steel, sharpened fingers at the edges plunging their barbs up into the sky.

Beyond him, the Rhine Valley brimmed, hills lapping out to the horizon: he snapped photos of all of it greedily.

Ascending of the tower proved a chore, but certainly worth the view. The city now blossomed below him, little tendrils of streets and waterlines falling away at all angles. It looked stunning in the ebb of the eve, so serene, so pristine, and he wondered for a minute what would happen as fall truly fell on this land, the little leaves giving way to sandy air, to longer nights. Again and again he nabbed shots, doing his best not to get to close to the edge of the platform. Symbology had found these twigs too, but no matter - on all sides, the land started to glow in a fever pitch of greens and reds. This he snapped at too.

Strange though - he had expected to see more people up here though, or else other photographers clicking way, jostling past each other for the best view. The tower was lovely in a way that made it a clickster's dream, asymmetrical, with little side-booths where people could mingle, frolic, could even kiss under the moonlight. Leave it to those backward Europeans to design something so beautiful, yet all so out of proportion with the human body – it hurt his head just to look at it, even more to move through it. Likely, it was just the exhaustion of the climb, the extra steps seeming a bit much alongside his weighted pack.

It looked like the sunset would be a bust, too, with long fingers of clouds seeming to come down now from the north. He flipped back through the photos, admiring his talent with a camera, but suddenly seeming a little strange, feeling as if the backgrounds were out of focus or something. He was just leaning in to examine closer, when the first of the loud sounds caught his ear.

KaBoom.

He stood for a bit, mesmerized, the land seeming to slosh a bit out beneath him. Though he had heard the wine of piccolo music most of the way up here, likely from the gypsy camp, this new sound almost sounded drum like, or else a hammers reverberation, quieting everything seeming for miles around. It shook the tower a tad as it went by, its echo's and sigh's carrying some cry, an energy, a charge he swore he could almost hear.

Was this ground seismic? He recalled the rebuilding efforts in that one medieval Swiss town to the south, but had no idea here. Perhaps the hill, hell, maybe the whole forest was a fault line?

Better to be down, he guessed, kicking himself, still feeling bewildered, still doing his best not to drop the pack, the camera, both.

Keee-rash, BaBoom.   BabaBabaBoom! More shifts, quieter that the first, but no less threatening. It was doing something to the base of his mind as well as the tower, waves and slows teetering back n forth. Wavering. Quicker his feet found treads.

It was when he was about halfway down from the tower that he realized what had nagged him at the summit. It hadn't been the light, nor the approaching nimbus that had bothered him then he realized, but something so much closer to his lens that he'd been mulling over. Yes, back home, such a sight, the peak, hell this entire tower would have been covered with children, dog walkers, people with snot clogging their faces as they laughed. Folks who would have been yelling obscenities, dealers in the corners, elders all looking for respite, bored teens, anything else than he had seen just moments before, on a sunny summer's eve, of all things.

Yes, no humanly sounds could he hear, no cough, sputter, or gaseous intake to humble him.

Also, what of the town?

He looked out and round, gasping now at the sights he *could* see, checking his camera rolodex again, furiously, wondering. Though the angle he was at now was a bit wrong, and though he could only see a few of the northmost streets, the digital display proved his uneasiness right. What he saw in hindsight, both from his lower vantage and in the cameras screen spooked him dearly. He peered closer into the histogram, expecting to see the thick tendrils of crowds milling about, crowds clogged with weekend traffic.

But no, the lens did not lie - they were suddenly all gone. White lights had begun to twinkle on, it was true, ghostly shadows reached as they fell, but the streets in all his pictures were empty. Everything seemed frozen, both on and off screen. Even with the height of summer near, the thrill of coming vacations, the streets he could witness and see were blank. The plaza's, the park, hell, even the square in front of the cathedral (which was always busy) seemed deserted, screen and view told him so. Derelict, even.

No honks, no calls, no outdoor music or city bells to tinkle upon the ears.

Gone, deserted.

For a full minute, he thought himself cast back in time, looking at a dead place growing in the pale screens light. Even the little river rivulets that crisscrossed the town seemed stuck, unyielding. He was flipping again through his screens, eyeing the mobile furiously, debating about calling the hotel, back home, anywhere, but then the beats started up in earnest again, matching his own heart thud.

Should he go up, above the tree line, to ensure the cameras accuracy?

No, no point. It was time to get down, time to get moving.

Boom, went another soft beat across the valley, as if to echo his thoughts.

The forest around him had begun to grow murky, quite dim; an optical effect he had not expected due to the thickened cloud cover. He was glad for an extra battery pack, happier still for his architectural memory of such twists and turns in the gloom, but it was this frenzied thinking and not seeing that almost got him into trouble. Without warning, he damn near ran into an old man standing silently on the trail, one leaning almost expectantly upward with the yew. Mitched bounced off of one of his shoulders, both annoyed and angry at the same time for the inconvenience, yet happy to see another human in all this waylaid green. He turned in his stumbling to greet him.

"Hey, sorry about that Mister," he tried in his terrible German, forgetting for a moment which city, which Bavarian state he was in. He was dusting himself off in a way, was reaching out to offer him a hand as the man shot him down.

"You might want to run, little man." The fellow said, speaking softly in a language Mitch did not at first understand.

"I, what?" Mitch tried, even a fell boom in the woods around him. They both looked toward the sound, which seemed everywhere and nowhere at once. The old man ahead of him looked ashen faced now, his thin German beard glistening with sweat. The ground swayed beneath them a tad, drumbeats sure and true.

"Time to run, I said." Mitch wanted to ask further, but the old man was now moving, was actually hurtling back behind him *up* the very slope he had come, something glistening in his hand.

Mitch didn't wait to be told, fleeing back down, down, to what he knew not.

Ahead, the trail branched out again. In his head, he could imagine fractals, spinning forever outward as he went - for which way now was true down? The paths before him turned, squirmed around as living things, leaving his nerves a short fork twirling round. His feet caught, the ground itself threatening to open up before him - oh God, he could feel the pounding, pulsing coming up from the ground. The thrumming coming through the very air behind him.

The bridge! Oh, how he had forgotten of that stupid thing. In his head, all the little lines, and the trail had suddenly become so jumbled together. Another boom reached his ears, sounding neither of treefall, nor of firecrackers, or of wood splintering into the dusk. It sounded like a heartbeat from the very bowels of the earth, coming up to shake his toes, nose all – how could he cross in such a state? He tossed the pack aside, started quickly over the fell beams. Kate would have given him much crap for his leavings, but he ignored such thoughts.

ABNOBA. He seemed to see the it everywhere now, little flakes and tendrils rising round. He could hear it in the thrum in the air. Saw now that the word had been carved into the steel beneath his hands he saw, the very shape of the bridge, of the tower, all, forming a giant letter "A" that wheeled skeletal into the night air. He pushed himself faster over the ruts, pausing at the halfway only as he realized everything had paused, somehow stopped, a whisper of a whisper seemed to be growing behind him.

"Hello?" He paused for a second, looking back in the silence of the eve, not sure what to expect. The canopy was split here, seeming somehow brighter, making his glance back through the struts strain his eyes.

He gave hope that it the old man, but recoiled at the sight nearing.

Someone, some *thing* was coming from back beyond alright, a long wave just visible in the darkness beneath the jungle trees. He leaned back, suddenly afraid, unsure of what to do. It (she?) was still waving, whether to beckon or jostle away, he was unsure. It, *they* had almost put a foot upon the first struts, before he found his composure, irked somehow about the manner of garment and dress, unsettled in his very lowest ebb.

"Hi!" said someone (something?) else at the same time, below him, and he almost screamed as he glanced down. The little ravine below had somehow also been filled with figures, most with similar wavery hair, all staring up, at him. Something about them looked mossy, ragged, and in moments they all had started to ascend the very canyon walls. Each uttering the same greeting as they climbed, all looking flattened, thickened, smiling at him.

He ran flat out now, unsure of what to do, or where to go. His feet flew over cracked wood, then finding gravel, gaining on the hardtop.

ABNOBA. He could hear it in the click of the air.

ABNOBA. Could hear the little tinkle of laughter coming from between the trees, from the very bushes he passed on lefts and rights, of hands pulling up and over the hardscape.

ABNOBA. The very ground had begun to pulse, the dirt itself sweating sound, seeming to flex in A's and O's and B's. Of feminine laughter, seeming to pulsate in the wood, gathering thick in the bracken round him. He trudged on, finding that the ethereal dark of the lower canopy, of the steeper slopes shifting down, down. He thought he could see eyes, and forms of many curves approaching. Features that all seemed slim, slanted, and he screamed again and again, breathless.

Left, right, down, down down. He didn't have time to check the map, everything becoming a blur.

He thought he could see eyes, and forms of many curves approaching.

ABNOBA. Another sign passing, this one new, he was sure. An arm jutting out of the dark, from around him, from behind the nearest tree, the same words cut, carved somehow into living flesh. Dodge, move, run. Run!

ABNOBA. They were whispering, saying something behind him. Gaining, he was sure. He tumbled on, on, feeling the next of the thick tree roots catching, pulling. He was too out of shape to go much longer, much further.

There.

He had reached an edge, a steep drop somehow, the frozen town suddenly at his feet, having no choice but to turn to face them or else risk a fall, his hands were bleeding now, cut on the branches smacking all around.

He turned, hands up, uncertain of what next to say, to do.

The first one was now there, pushing through, standing tall, fast, making some sort of sign in the air, reaching for him in a manner he almost swore he knew. He waved his hands in front of his own face, stepping back, away, trying to apologize, trying to say anything. To plead, to be away from that glance he swore he knew, she, it, they were all coming closer, saying the same thing over and over endlessly, him stepping back, stepping further away, stepping, he….

Then was tumbling down, down, forever down, out back over the lip of the drop.

He. He. He fell.

He rolled.

He had landed flat on his back in the park, wind knocked completely out of him, crawling his way forward, further down, out into the main street of the town, bodies suddenly everywhere around him.

At first he recoiled from them, seeing wide hands and gaping mouths that reminded him too much of the forest for first glance. Their faces were too dark, he forgetting that the sun was mostly gone, distant somewhere. Yet the sun *did* seem to have one last little trick, sliding out for a moment from the tepid cloud clover to turn everything bright reds and golds in the area around him, if only for a moment, making him pause, making him fall further still. At first he recoiled from them, seeing wide hands and gaping mouths that reminded him too much of the forest for first glance. Their faces were too dark, him forgetting that the woods, everything; that the edge was gone.

Yet then true twilight found them all, as a large fraulein was jostling toward him, reaching for a kerchief as she came, darkness seeming to envelop all. Then others too were nearing, a look of concern upon their brows, nearing further still. He waved again and again at them, uncertain, but still they pressed onward, toward him, arms reaching.

As the townsfolk rushed in, he collapsed, looking up at the strange canopy that wheeled overhead, listening only to the fading voices, the gasps of the townsfolk as they pointed, gasped.

"There's something....something up...on the hill..." he tried, looking up, far too up towards where the nearest face approached him, realizing too late that they might be here to help. In his rush to speak he had forgotten what little German he knew, resorting back to the plain-speak of points and grunts. The sky was different, stronger here, the same constellations meaningless under a opening sky.

The fraulein merely looked down at him through all of this, then up to the peak of the park, where he (she?) made a sign to themselves, seeming to understand something beyond his reckoning.

Cold, so cold he thought, turning his face down, turning what remained inward, down, down, further still.

Above him, true night was drifting in.

Meanwhile, people did their best not to stair too long out their windows, at the sight now filling the square. In time, they dragged the visitor outward, onward, continuing to cross themselves, staring every now and again toward the wood, glad to be inside, if only for one night.

ABNOBA.

Around them, the night continued to settle unabated. Time seemed to stand still - for a little while, at least.

—— FIN ——

Milton Keynes UK
Ingram Content Group UK Ltd.
UKHW021823121023
430461UK00016B/431